MILLY-MOLLY-MANDY'S

Autumn

Milly-Molly-Mandy books

Joyce Lankester Brisley

MILLY-MOLLY-MANDY'S Autumn

MACMILLAN CHILDREN'S BOOKS

The stories in this collection first appeared in
Further Doings of Milly-Molly-Mandy (1932)
Milly-Molly-Mandy Again (1948)
Milly-Molly-Mandy & Co. (1955)
Published by George G. Harrap & Co. Ltd

This edition published 2012 by Macmillan Children's Books
a division of Macmillan Publishers Limited
20 New Wharf Road, London N1 9RR
Basingstoke and Oxford
Associated companies throughout the world
www.panmacmillan.com

ISBN 978-1-4472-0801-3

A CIP catalogue record for this book is available from the British Library.

Printed and bound in China

Publisher's Note
*The stories in this collection are reproduced in the form in which they appeared
upon first publication in the UK by George G. Harrap & Co. Ltd.
All spellings remain consistent with these original editions.*

Contents

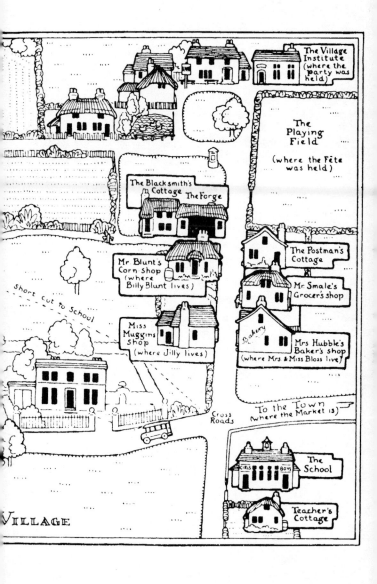

The Village Institute (where the party was held)

The Playing Field (where the Fête was held)

The Blacksmith's Cottage   The Forge

The Postman's Cottage

Mr Smale's Grocer's shop

Mr Blunt's Corn Shop (where Billy Blunt lives)

Short cut to School

Miss Muggins Shop (where Jilly lives)

Bakery

Mrs Hubble's Baker's shop (where Mrs & Miss Bloss live)

To the Town (where the Market is)

Cross Roads

GIRLS   BOYS   The School

Teacher's Cottage

VILLAGE

Milly-Molly-Mandy and the Surprise Plant

Once upon a time Milly-Molly-Mandy was busy in her own little garden beside the nice white cottage with the thatched roof, planting radish seeds.

Milly-Molly-Mandy's father grew all sorts of vegetables in his big garden – potatoes and turnips and cabbages and peas, which Father and Mother and Grandpa and Grandma and Uncle and Aunty and Milly-Molly-Mandy ate every day for dinner. And he grew fruit too – gooseberries and raspberries and currants and apples, which Mother made into jams and puddings and pies for them all. But, somehow, nothing ever tasted *quite* so good as the things which grew in Milly-Molly-Mandy's own little garden!

There wasn't much room in it, of course, so she could grow only small things, like radishes, or spring-onions, or lettuces, and mostly there wasn't enough of them to give more than a tiny taste each to such a big family as Milly-Molly-Mandy's. But every one enjoyed those tiny tastes extra specially much, so that they always seemed to be a real feast!

Well, this time Milly-Molly-Mandy was planting quite a number of seeds, because she thought it would be nice to have enough radishes to give at least two each to Father and Mother and Grandpa and Grandma and Uncle and Aunty and perhaps to little-friend-Susan and Billy Blunt, and, of course, Milly-Molly-Mandy her own self. (How many's that?)

She was just crumbling earth finely with her fingers to cover up the seeds, when who should come along the road but Mr Rudge the Blacksmith, looking very clean and tidy. (He was going for a walk with the young lady who helped Mrs Hubble in the Baker's shop.)

"Hullo, Mr Rudge," said Milly-Molly-Mandy, looking up at him over the hedge.

"Hullo, there!" said Mr Rudge, looking down at her over the hedge. "What's this I see – some one digging the garden with her nose?"

"I don't dig with my nose!" said Milly-Molly-Mandy. "I'm planting radish seeds, with my hands. But my nose tickled and – I rubbed it. Is it muddy?"

"That's all right," said the Blacksmith. "I always notice things grow best for people who get muddy noses. Well, what's it going to be this time?"

"Radishes," said Milly-Molly-Mandy. "A lot of them. For Father and Mother and Grandpa and Grandma and Uncle and Aunty. And some over – I hope."

"Bless my boots!" said the Blacksmith. "You've got a family to feed, no mistake. You ought to try growing something like – Now, wait a minute! I believe I've got an idea. Supposing I were to give you a plant; have you got any room for it?"

"What sort of a plant?" asked Milly-Molly-Mandy with interest.

"It's some I'm growing myself, and I've got one to spare. I don't believe your dad's got any, so you'd have it all to yourself."

"Is it something you can eat?" asked Milly-Molly-Mandy.

"Rather! – puddings, pies, what-not," said the Blacksmith.

"Enough for Father and Mother and Grandpa and Grandma and Uncle and

Aunty?" said Milly-Molly-Mandy.

"Yes, and you too."

"Could it go in there?" asked Milly-Molly-Mandy excitedly, pointing to a space beside the radish seeds. "There's nothing in there yet. How big is the plant?"

"Oh, about *so* big," said the Blacksmith, holding his hands five or six inches apart. "It'll want a good rich soil. Got any rotten grass-cuttings?"

"Father has, I think," said Milly-Molly-Mandy, "he puts it in a heap over there to rot."

"Well, you ask him to let you have some, quite a nice lot, and put it on the earth there, and I'll bring you along the plant to-morrow. It's a surprise plant – you stick it in and see what'll happen."

"Thank you very much, Mr Rudge," said Milly-Molly-Mandy, wondering whatever it could be.

Mr Rudge the Blacksmith went on down the road with the young lady (who had been patiently waiting all this time), and Milly-Molly-Mandy ran to ask Father if she could have some of the rotten grass-cuttings. He brought her some spadefuls (it was all brown and messy and didn't look the least bit like grass, but he said it was just how plants liked it), and she dug it into the space beside the radish seeds and hoped Mr Rudge wouldn't forget about the Surprise Plant.

And Mr Rudge didn't.

The very next evening, when he'd done banging horse-shoes on his anvil with a great big hammer, he took off his leather apron and shut up his forge; and presently Milly-Molly-Mandy, who was looking out for him, saw him coming along up the road. He'd got the plant with its roots in a lump of earth wrapped in thick paper in his pocket.

Milly-Molly-Mandy helped him to take it out very carefully. And then he helped Milly-Molly-Mandy to plant it in the space beside the radish seeds.

And there it stood, looking rather important all by itself (because, of course, the radishes weren't up yet).

"It'll want a lot of water, mind," said the Blacksmith, as he went out of the gate back to his supper, which he said was waiting for him. So Milly-Molly-Mandy said yes, good-bye, and thank you, and then she went and told Father about it.

Father came and looked at the plant very carefully (it had two rough scratchy leaves and two smooth seed-leaves). And Father said, "A Surprise Plant, is it? Well, well!"

Then Mother came out and

she looked at the plant, and she said, "Isn't it a marrow?"

But Milly-Molly-Mandy was quite sure it wasn't a marrow because Mr Rudge had said that Father hadn't got any like this in his garden, and Father had lots of marrows.

Well, the Surprise Plant soon felt at home, and it began to GROW.

The radishes started to come up, but the Surprise Plant came faster. It spread out branches along the earth, with tendrils which curled round any stalk or twig they met and held fast. Soon it covered all the radishes with its great green scratchy leaves, and filled up all Milly-Molly-Mandy's little garden.

Then it began to open big yellow flowers here and there, so that Milly-Molly-Mandy called out, "Oh, come quick and look at my Surprise Flowers!" and Father and Mother and Grandpa and Grandma and Uncle and Aunty came to look.

Father said, "Well, it seems to be getting on all right!"

And Mother said, "Surely it's a marrow!"

And Grandpa said, "No, 'tisn't a marrow."

And Grandma said, "It's got much the same sort of flower as a marrow."

And Uncle said, "You'll soon see what it is!"

And Aunty said, "Whatever it is, it looks as if Milly-Molly-Mandy will be giving us a good big taste this time!"

But Milly-Molly-Mandy said, "I don't see what there is to *eat* here – and there won't be any radishes now, because they're all hidden up in leaves."

After a while Milly-Molly-Mandy noticed that one of the flowers had a sort of round yellow ball below the petals, just where the stalk joins on; and as the flower faded the ball began to grow bigger.

She brought Mother to look at it.

Mother said at once, "Why! I know what it is now!"

Milly-Molly-Mandy said, "*What?*"

And Mother said, "Of course! It's a pumpkin!"

"Oh-h-h!" said Milly-Molly-Mandy.

Fancy! – a real pumpkin, like what Cinderella went to the ball in drawn by mice, growing in Milly-Molly-Mandy's own little garden!

"Oh-h!" said Milly-Molly-Mandy again.

She didn't mind now if the radishes were spoiled — but anyhow enough came up to give one little red one each to Father and Mother and Grandpa and Grandma and Uncle and Aunty and a weeny one for Milly-Molly-Mandy herself (and how many's that?) — for just think! soon she would be able to go out into her very own little garden and cut a great big pumpkin for them!

Father and Mother and Grandpa and Grandma and Uncle and Aunty began to say, "How's your coach getting on, Cinderella?" when they met her; and Uncle pretended he'd just seen a mouse running that way to gallop off with it to the ball!

It was a lovely hot summer, which was just what the pumpkin liked (as well as Milly-Molly-Mandy), and it grew and it grew. And do you know, other little pumpkin-balls grew under other flowers too, and two of them grew so big that Father gave Milly-Molly-Mandy some straw to put on the ground underneath, for them to rest on. But the first pumpkin grew biggest.

When Mr Rudge the Blacksmith passed along that way he always stopped to look over the hedge, and he said her pumpkin was bigger than any of his own!

Well, September came, and corn was cut, and apples were picked, and the yearly Harvest Festival was to be held in the Village Church. Grown-ups sent in their gifts the day before, to decorate the Church, but the children were to have a special Service in the afternoon, and bring their own offerings then.

Father sent in a big marrow and some of his best pears. Mother sent some pots of jam. Grandpa sent a large bunch of late roses. Grandma sent a little cream-cheese.

Uncle sent a basket of nice brown eggs. Aunty sent some bunches of lavender.

And what do you suppose Milly-Molly-Mandy took to the Children's Service?

Well, first she looked at her pumpkins, the great big one and the second-best one. And then she said to Mother, "Mother, what is a Harvest Festival for? – why do you send fruit and things to Church?"

Mother said, "It's to say 'thank you' to God for giving us such a lot of good things."

"But what becomes of them, those apples, and the jam?" asked Milly-Molly-Mandy.

"Vicar sends them to the Cottage Hospital generally, so the people there can enjoy them."

"Does God like that, when they're given to Him?" asked Milly-Molly-Mandy.

"Yes," said Mother. "He takes the *giving* part, the being thankful part, and the rest Vicar sends to people who need it most, so it's a double giving."

"Well, I'm very thankful indeed for lots of things!" said Milly-Molly-Mandy. "So hadn't I better give my pumpkin? We could eat the second-best one and the other little ones ourselves, couldn't we?"

So on the Sunday afternoon they all walked across the fields to Church, in their best clothes, Father and Mother and Grandpa and Grandma and Uncle and Aunty and Milly-Molly-Mandy – AND the pumpkin. She had cut through its stalk herself with a big knife (Father helping), and cleaned it carefully with a damp cloth (Mother helping), and it was so big and heavy that Father had to carry it for her till they came to the Church.

There was quite a number of children carrying things in: little-friend-Susan had a bunch of flowers from her garden, marigolds and Michaelmas-daisies, and

On Sunday afternoon they all walked to Church

nasturtiums, and Billy Blunt brought a basket of little yellow apples which grew by their back fence.

Milly-Molly-Mandy sat in a pew, next to Mother, looking over the big pumpkin in her lap till the time came to give it up.

And then all the children walked in a line to the front of the Church, and Vicar took their gifts one after another and laid them out on a table.

Milly-Molly-Mandy was so pleased to have such a beautiful pumpkin to give that when she had got rid of the big burden she ran hoppity-skip back up the aisle, forgetting she was in Church till she saw Mother's face smiling but making a silent "Ssh!" to her. And then she slid quietly into her seat, and sat admiring the things decorating the Church – the bunches of corn, and fancy loaves of bread (she guessed Mrs Hubble the Baker had sent those), the baskets of fruit and vegetables and flowers and eggs, and pots of preserves with the sun shining through them.

And the pumpkin lay, smooth and round and yellow, among the other things which the children had brought. (But somehow it didn't look quite so awfully big and important there in Church as it had done at home!)

When the service was over everybody went home. And at tea-time Mother said, "This week I ought to make some more jam. I was thinking how very nice it would be if we could have pumpkin-and-ginger jam this year, as a change from marrow-and-ginger!"

Then they all looked hopefully at Milly-Molly-Mandy.

And Milly-Molly-Mandy said at once, "Yes! It would! Shall I go and cut my

17

second-best pumpkin now? And the other little pumpkins?"

So that week Mother made lots of pots of pumpkin-and-ginger jam, Milly-Molly-Mandy helping. And on Saturday Mother let her ask little-friend-Susan and Billy Blunt to tea, and they all had pumpkin-and-ginger jam on their bread-and-butter (as well as chocolate cake and currant buns).

And Father and Mother and Grandpa and Grandma and Uncle and Aunty and little-friend-Susan and Billy Blunt and her own self all thought it was the very best jam they had ever tasted.

And the next time she saw Mr Rudge the Blacksmith, Milly-Molly-Mandy gave him a little pot of pumpkin jam all to himself, to say thank-you-for-giving-me-the-Surprise-Plant.

Milly-Molly-Mandy Cooks a Dinner

Once upon a time Milly-Molly-Mandy was coming home after morning school with little-friend-Susan and Billy Blunt.

They were all talking about what they might be going to have for their dinners (feeling very hungry at that time, of course), and about the sort of things they liked and the sort of things they didn't like.

Billy Blunt said he didn't like turnips or parsnips, and little-friend-Susan said she didn't like potatoes or carrots. Milly-Molly-Mandy said what she didn't like was stew, with bits of meat and vegetables floating in it. And Billy Blunt and little-friend-Susan agreed that that was just what they didn't like either. They all hoped none of them would have stew for dinner that day!

(They needn't have worried, for none of them did.)

The next day was Saturday, and there was no school. So Milly-Molly-Mandy stayed around the nice white cottage with the thatched roof, helping Father in the garden.

Father was very busy, digging up potatoes and cutting down dead plants and burning rubbish on a big bonfire. So Milly-Molly-Mandy was very busy too, sweeping up leaves and picking up tools which Father dropped and throwing bits on to the bonfire.

(Autumn is a very busy time in a garden.)

Presently   little-friend-Susan   came

wandering up the road, wondering what Milly-Molly-Mandy was doing. She saw the smoke, so she peeped over the hedge outside the nice white cottage with the thatched roof.

"Hullo, Susan!" called Milly-Molly-Mandy. "Look at our bonfire! You'd better come and help me to help Father!"

So little-friend-Susan ran in at the gate and round to the back garden. And soon the two of them were very busy, throwing bits on to the bonfire.

Presently Billy Blunt came wandering up the road, wondering (rather) what Milly-Molly-Mandy was doing. He saw the smoke too, and looked over the hedge outside the nice white cottage with the thatched roof.

"Hullo, Billy!" called Milly-Molly-Mandy. "Look, it's a bonfire! Come and help us to help Father!"

So Billy Blunt walked in at the gate and round to the back garden. And soon all three of them were very busy throwing bits on to the bonfire.

(But somehow, Father thought, three people together weren't half so helpful as one person alone!)

The bonfire puffed big, beautiful clouds of smoke out, and, whichever side they stood it seemed trying to puff right into their faces. Milly-Molly-Mandy and little-friend-Susan and Billy Blunt had to keep running round to one side or another as they threw on bits of twig and dead leaves.

"Tell you what," said Billy Blunt, after a

while, "if we had some chestnuts we could roast them."

But they hadn't any chestnuts so they couldn't.

"I wonder what else there is we could cook," said Milly-Molly-Mandy, looking about.

And then she noticed a heap of straggly old bean-plants waiting to be burned, and they had a few big bean-pods still hanging on here and there.

"Oh look!" said Milly-Molly-Mandy; "perfectly good beans!"

"Can't we cook them?" said little-friend-Susan.

"You can't eat those," said Billy Blunt. "Too old."

"Maybe you can't eat them at table," said Milly-Molly-Mandy, "but if we cook them ourselves on the bonfire maybe we could!"

So they all searched for bean-pods and opened them, and they got quite a handful of lovely big purple-speckled beans.

"What do we cook them in?" said Milly-Molly-Mandy.

"They'll need a lot of boiling," said little-friend-Susan.

"You want a tin can, like tramps have!" said Billy Blunt.

That was a bright idea. So Milly-Molly-Mandy ran indoors to ask Mother, and Mother gave her an empty treacle-tin with a lid. They washed it well under the pump, and put the beans in with some clean water, and set it on the bonfire to boil. They had to watch it, because when the fire blazed up the tin fell over, and Billy Blunt had to rescue it with the gardening-fork. It boiled till the lid blew off. And then Billy Blunt (who was beginning to feel hungry) said:

"I should think they're done now."

So they emptied the tin out on to the ground and divided the beans. They were quite soft inside, so they peeled the skins off, and ate them rather like chestnuts. They did enjoy them!

When Father came along with another load of weeds and brambles to put on the bonfire and saw what they were doing, he said:

"Ah, if you want real gipsy cooking

there's nothing to beat a good hot potato, baked in its jacket!" And he pointed to the wheelbarrow full of newly dug potatoes, and added, "Help yourselves – only don't waste them."

Milly-Molly-Mandy and little-friend-Susan and Billy Blunt were pleased! They helped themselves to two potatoes each, and Father showed how to bury them in the hot ashes under the bonfire.

"You'll have to leave them for a good half-hour and more," he said, as he went off.

It seemed an awfully long time to wait. They were all feeling very hungry by now.

"Tell you what," said Billy Blunt, "we ought to get some salt and butter to eat with those potatoes when they're done."

"Oo, yes!" said little-friend-Susan, "we ought."

"Let's ask Mother," said Milly-Molly-Mandy.

So they went into the kitchen, where Mother was putting a pie into the oven and Aunty was laying the table.

"Please," said Milly-Molly-Mandy, "could we have just a bit of butter and salt to eat with our baked potatoes out there?"

"Goodness me!" said Mother. "Whatever next?"

"They'll spoil their dinners next," said Aunty.

"Oh, we won't – truly – we're so dreadfully hungry!" said Milly-Molly-Mandy.

And little-friend-Susan and Billy Blunt said: "Yes, we are!"

"But dinner will be ready in half an hour," said Mother.

"Oh, dear – so will our potatoes be!" said Milly-Molly-Mandy.

"They're cooking under the bonfire," said little-friend-Susan.

"We're not to waste them," said Billy Blunt.

Then Milly-Molly-Mandy had a bright idea.

"Mother, couldn't you let us cook our own dinners all by ourselves out on the bonfire, just for once? It would be such fun! Please! Couldn't we, Mother?"

"Yes!" said little-friend-Susan and Billy Blunt.

"But what would your mothers say if you don't go home to a proper dinner?" Mother asked them.

"We could go and ask," said little-friend-Susan and Billy Blunt at once.

"Well," said Mother, "if Mrs Moggs and Mrs Blunt don't object I suppose you may, just this once."

So little-friend-Susan and Billy Blunt rushed off to ask permission while Milly-Molly-Mandy borrowed a saucepan (one that didn't matter very much), and some old cooking-plates and spoons, and some bread, and salt, and butter (margarine really).

Mother gave her some scraps of meat, and told her to help herself to whichever vegetables she wanted from the box in the scullery. So Milly-Molly-Mandy helped herself to some of everything – onions, carrots, parsnips – and carried all outside in readiness.

Very soon little-friend-Susan came running back, saying her mother didn't mind if Milly-Molly-Mandy's mother didn't. And she brought a strip of bacon in a paper.

Then Billy Blunt came panting back (he had farther to go), saying his mother made no objection if he chose to miss a proper dinner this once. And he brought a sausage on an old fork.

Father had made the bonfire burn up till it was mostly just a heap of red-hot ashes now. Then he went indoors to have his dinner. And the three of them stayed outdoors, and got to work cooking their own.

Milly-Molly-Mandy cut up vegetables into the saucepan, with scraps of meat and some water, and set it on top of the fire to boil. Little-friend-Susan toasted bacon on a stick. And Billy Blunt toasted sausage on a fork.

Then they remembered the potatoes, and Milly-Molly-Mandy started poking about in the ashes. Little-friend-Susan was so busy watching her that she let her bacon catch fire; and Billy Blunt was so busy grinning to see her blowing it out that he didn't notice his own sausage burning until the others shouted at him! After a good scraping the bit of bacon and the sausage were added to the stew to finish cooking while the potatoes were got out.

"Aren't they beautifully done!" said Milly-Molly-Mandy, brushing their skins on the grass.

"Aren't they hot!" said little-friend-Susan, sucking her fingers.

"Let's begin!" said Billy Blunt.

So, as they were all frightfully hungry by now and the stew wasn't quite done, they each took a hot baked potato in their hands and broke it open, and put in a dab of butter and a pinch of salt, and ate it out of its skin – like that, standing round the bonfire.

And, my! you never tasted anything so good as those potatoes!

"It's made me hungrier than ever," said Billy Blunt, when he had eaten his two.

So then they couldn't wait any longer. They took the saucepan off the fire and spooned stew out on to the plates. It tasted rather of bonfire smoke, and they had forgotten the salt, and the vegetables were a bit hard.

But, my! you *never* tasted anything so good as that stew!

And, as Billy Blunt said, "It's good for your teeth to bite up well. Too much soft food's bad."

So they all bit up very well indeed, dividing everything equally down to the last scrap.

They each took a hot baked potato

One thing is very certain, Grandma would have said that "Mr Manners' didn't get much of a look-in at that meal. (But then, you couldn't expect to find "Mr Manners' anywhere around in so much bonfire smoke!)

"Well," said Milly-Molly-Mandy at last, "we can't say we don't like stew, or carrots, or potatoes, or parsnips now!"

"Ah," said Billy Blunt, "but we never have stew like this at home!"

"I wish," said little-friend-Susan, "we

could always cook our dinners ourselves. It would save a lot of washing up, too."

Just then Mother looked out of the back door.

"What about finishing up this treacle-tart, though you haven't cooked it yourselves?" she called.

Well, of course, you couldn't say no to Mother's treacle-tart. So they managed to find enough room, but only just! Then, sticky, greasy, smoky, and very comfortable inside, they carried their things indoors to be washed up.

But – do you know! – there seemed to be more washing up to be done than they had supposed. For, besides their plates and spoons and the saucepan, there were – Milly-Molly-Mandy and little-friend-Susan and Billy Blunt!

(And they took a good deal of washing up, I can tell you!)

Milly-Molly-Mandy and the Blacksmith's Wedding

Once upon a time Milly-Molly-Mandy was going to a wedding.

It wasn't just the ordinary sort of wedding, where you stared through the churchyard railings, wondering at ladies walking outdoors in their party clothes and who the man in the tight collar was.

This was a very important wedding indeed.

Mr Rudge the Blacksmith was marrying the young lady who helped in Mrs Hubble the Baker's shop. AND (which Milly-Molly-Mandy thought the most important part) there were to be two bridesmaids. And the bridesmaids were Milly-Molly-Mandy and little-friend-Susan.

Milly-Molly-Mandy was sorry that Billy Blunt couldn't be a bridesmaid too, but Billy Blunt said he didn't care because *he* thought the most important part came later.

In the Village, in olden days, when the blacksmith or any of his family got married, he used to "fire the anvil" outside his forge, with real gunpowder, to celebrate! That's what Mr Rudge the Blacksmith said. He said his father had been married that way, and his uncle, and both his aunts, and his grandpa, and his great-grandpa a long time back. And that was how he meant to be married too, quite properly.

Billy Blunt didn't think many blacksmiths could be properly married, for he had never seen a blacksmith's wedding before, nor even *heard* one, and neither had Milly-Molly-Mandy, nor little-friend-Susan.

Anyhow, though he wasn't a bridesmaid, Billy Blunt had a proper invitation to the wedding, like Mr and Mrs Blunt (Billy Blunt's father and mother), and Mr and Mrs Moggs (little-friend-Susan's father and mother), and Milly-Molly-Mandy's Father and Mother and Grandpa and Grandma and Uncle and Aunty, and some other important friends. (For, of course, only important friends get proper invitations to weddings; the other sort have to peep through the railings or hang round by the lane.)

Well, it was only a few days to the wedding now, and Milly-Molly-Mandy and little-friend-Susan and Billy Blunt were coming home from afternoon school. And when they came to the corn-shop (where Billy Blunt lived) they could hear *clink-clang* noises coming from the Forge near by; so they all went round by the lane to have a look in. (For nobody can pass near a forge when things are going on without wanting to look in.)

Mr Rudge the Blacksmith was mending a plough, which wasn't quite so interesting to watch as shoeing a horse, but there was a nice piece of red-hot metal being hammered and bent to the right shape. The great iron hammer bounced off each time, as if it knew just how hot the metal was and didn't want to stay there long, and the iron anvil rang so loudly at every bang and bounce that the Blacksmith couldn't hear anyone speak. But presently he turned and buried the metal in his fire to heat it again, and the Blacksmith's Boy began working the handle of the bellows up and down till the flames roared and sparks flew.

It was just quiet enough then for Milly-Molly-Mandy to call out:

"Hullo, Mr Rudge."

And Mr Rudge said, "Hullo, there! Been turned out of school again, have you? Go on, Reginald, push her up."

So the boy pushed harder at the handle, and the fire roared and the sparks flew.

"Is that really his name?" asked Milly-Molly-Mandy.

"My name's Tom," said the boy, pumping away.

"Can't have two Toms here," said the Blacksmith.

"That's my name. He'll have to be content

with Reginald. Now then, out of the way, there!"

They all scattered in a hurry as the Blacksmith brought the piece of metal glowing hot out of the fire with his long-handled tongs, and laid it on the anvil again, and began to drill screw-holes in it. The drill seemed to go through the red-hot iron as easily as if it were cheese. As it cooled off and turned grey and hard again, the Blacksmith put it back into the fire. So then they could talk some more.

"Where do you put the gunpowder when you fire the anvil?" asked Billy Blunt.

"In that hole, there," said the Blacksmith, pointing at his anvil.

So Billy Blunt and Milly-Molly-Mandy and little-friend-Susan bent over to see. And, sure enough, there was a small square hole in the top of the anvil. (You look at an anvil if you get the chance, and see.)

"That won't hold very much," said little-friend-Susan, quite disappointed.

"It'll hold a famous big bang – you just wait," said the Blacksmith. "You don't want me to blow up all the lot of you, do you?"

"Have you got the gunpowder ready?" asked Milly-Molly-Mandy.

"I have," said Mr Rudge.

"Where do you keep it?" asked little-friend-Susan, looking about.

"Not just around here, I can tell you that much," said Mr Rudge.

"Where do you get gunpowder?" asked Billy Blunt.

But the Blacksmith said he wasn't giving away any secrets like that. And he brought the piece of metal out of the fire and started hammering again.

When he had put it back into the fire Milly-Molly-Mandy said:

"Aunty has nearly finished making our bridesmaids' dresses, Mr Rudge."

"I should hope so!" said the Blacksmith. "How do you suppose I'm to be married next Saturday if you bridesmaids aren't ready? Go on, Reginald, get a move on."

"They're long dresses, almost down to our feet," said little-friend-Susan. "But we're to have a lot of tucks put in them afterwards, so that we can wear them for

Sunday-best. And when we grow the tucks can be let out."

"That's an idea," said the Blacksmith. "I'll ask for tucks to be put in my wedding suit, so that I can wear it for Sunday-best afterwards."

Whereupon the Blacksmith's Boy burst out laughing so loudly, as he worked the bellows, that he made more noise than the other three all put together.

The Blacksmith fished the red-hot metal from the fire, and plunged it for a second into a tank of water near by, and there was a great hissing and steaming, and a lot of queer smell.

"What do you do that for?" asked Billy Blunt.

"Tempers the iron," said the Blacksmith, trying it against the plough to see if it fitted properly; "brisks it up, like when you have a cold bath on a hot day."

He laid it on the anvil, and took up a smaller hammer and began tapping away. So Milly-Molly-Mandy and little-friend-Susan and Billy Blunt thought perhaps it was time to go now, so they said good-bye and went off home to their teas.

And Milly-Molly-Mandy and little-friend-Susan had another trying-on of their bridesmaids' dresses after tea. And Aunty stitched and stitched away, so that they should be ready in time for the wedding.

Well, the great day came. And Milly-Molly-Mandy and little-friend-Susan, dressed alike in long pink dresses with bunches of roses in their hands, followed the young lady who helped Mrs Hubble the Baker up the aisle of the Church, to where Mr Rudge the Blacksmith was waiting.

Mr Rudge looked so clean in his new

navy blue suit with shiny white collar and cuffs and a big white button-hole, that Milly-Molly-Mandy hardly knew him (though she had seen him clean before, when he played cricket on the playing-field, or walked out with the young lady who helped Mrs Hubble the Baker).

Then, when the marrying was done, Milly-Molly-Mandy and little-friend-Susan followed the Bride and Bridegroom down the aisle to the door, while everybody in the pews smiled and smiled, and Miss Bloss, who played the harmonium behind a red curtain, played so loudly and cheerfully, and Reginald the Blacksmith's Boy who pumped the bellows for her (so he did a lot of pumping one way and another) pushed the handle up and down so vigorously, it's a wonder they didn't burst the harmonium between them. (But they didn't often have a wedding to play for.)

Then the two Bridesmaids, with the Bride and Bridegroom, of course, stood outside on the Church step to be photographed.

Then everybody walked in a procession down the lane, past the Blacksmith's house and past the Forge (which was closed), and up the road to the Inn, where a room had been hired for the wedding-breakfast (though it was early afternoon).

And then everybody stood around eating and drinking and making jokes and laughing and making speeches and clapping and laughing a lot more.

And Milly-Molly-Mandy and little-friend-Susan and Billy Blunt ate and laughed and clapped as much as anyone (though I'm not sure if Billy Blunt laughed as much as the others, as he was so busy "sampling" things).

They had two ice-creams each (as

They stood on the Church step to be photographed

Grandma and one or two others didn't want theirs), and they had a big slice of wedding cake each, as well as helpings of nearly everything else, because Mr Rudge insisted on their having it, though their mothers said they'd had quite enough. (He was a very nice man!)

And THEN came the great moment when everybody came out of the Inn and went to the Forge to fire the anvil.

Mr Rudge unlocked the big doors and fastened them back. And then he and Father and Uncle and Mr Blunt and Mr Smale the Grocer between them pulled and pushed the heavy anvil outside into the lane. (The anvil had been cleaned up specially, so it didn't make their hands as dirty as you might think.)

And then Mr Rudge put some black powder into the little square hole in the anvil (Billy Blunt didn't see where he got it from). And the men-folk arranged a long piece of cord (which they called the fuse) from the hole down on to the ground. And then Mr Rudge took a box of matches from his pocket, and struck one, and set the end of the fuse alight.

And then everybody ran back and made a big half-circle round the front of the Forge and waited.

Mother and Mrs Moggs and Mrs Blunt wanted Milly-Molly-Mandy and little-friend-Susan and Billy Blunt to keep near them, and Mr Rudge kept by the young lady who used to help Mrs Hubble the Baker (but she wasn't going to any more, as she was Mrs Rudge now, and Mr Rudge said she'd have her work cut out looking after him). She seemed very frightened and held her hands over her ears, so he kept his arm round her.

Milly-Molly-Mandy and little-friend-

Susan put their hands half over their ears and hopped up and down excitedly. But Billy Blunt put his hands in his pockets and stood quite still. He said he didn't want to waste any of the bang.

The little flame crept along the fuse, nearer and nearer. And it began to creep up the anvil. And they all waited, breathless, for the big bang. They waited. And they waited.

And they waited.

"What's the matter with the thing?" said Mr Rudge, taking his arm away from the young lady who was Mrs Rudge now. "Has the fuse gone out? Keep back, everybody, it isn't safe yet."

So they waited some more. But still nothing happened.

At last Mr Rudge walked over to the anvil, and so did the other men (though the women didn't want them to).

"Ha!" said Mr Rudge. "Fuse went out just as it reached the edge of the anvil. Now what'll we do? It's too short to re-light."

"I've got some string," said Billy Blunt, and he rummaged in his breeches pocket.

"Bring it here, and let's have a look at it," said Mr Rudge.

So Billy Blunt went close and gave it to him (and took a good look into the hole at the same time).

"Will that carry the flame, d'you think?" said Father.

"Might do, if you give it a rub with a bit of candle-wax," said Mr Smale the Grocer.

"I think I've got a bit of wax," said Billy Blunt, rummaging in his pocket again.

"Hand it over," said Mr Rudge. "What else have you got in there – a general store?"

"It's bees'-wax, not candle-wax,

though," said Billy Blunt.

"It's got a bit stuck," said Billy Blunt, still rummaging.

"You boys – whatever will you put in your pockets next?" said Mrs Blunt.

"Better turn it inside out," said Uncle.

So Billy Blunt pulled his whole pocket outside. And there *was* a lot of things in it – marbles, and horse-chestnuts, and putty, and a pocket-knife, and a pencil holder, and a broken key, and a ha'penny, and several bus tickets, and some other things. And stuck half into the lining at the seam was a lump of bees'-wax, which they dug off with the pocket-knife.

"You have your uses, William," said Mr Rudge. And he waxed the string, and arranged it to hang from the anvil along the ground. And he struck a match and lit the end. And everybody ran back again in a hurry, and made a big half-circle round the anvil, and waited as before.

And the little flame crept along, and it paused and looked as if it were going out, and it crept on again, and it reached the anvil, an it began to creep up, and everybody waited, and Milly-Molly-Mandy and little-friend-Susan put their hands over their ears and smiled at each other, and Billy Blunt put his hands deep in his pockets and frowned straight ahead.

And the little flame crept up the string to the top of the anvil, and everybody held their breath, and Milly-Molly-Mandy pressed her hands hard over her ears, and then she was afraid she might not hear enough so she lifted them off – and, just at

that very moment, there came a great big
enormous

BANG!

And Milly-Molly-Mandy and little-
friend-Susan jumped and gave a shriek
because they were so splendidly startled
(even though they were expecting it). And
Billy Blunt grinned and looked pleased.
And everybody began to talk and exclaim
together as they went forward to look at
the anvil (which wasn't hurt at all, only a

bit dirty-looking round the hole).

Then everybody shook hands with the Blacksmith and his Bride, and told them they certainly had been properly married, and wished them well. And the Blacksmith thanked them all heartily.

And when it came time for Milly-Molly-Mandy and little-friend-Susan and Billy blunt to shake hands and say thank-you-for-a-nice-wedding-party, Mr Rudge said:

"Well, now, what sort of a wedding it would have been without you bridesmaids, and Billy Blunt to provide all our requirements out of his ample pockets, I just cannot conceive!"

And everybody laughed, and Mr Rudge smacked Billy Blunt on the shoulder so that he nearly fell over (but it didn't hurt him).

So then Milly-Molly-Mandy and little-friend-Susan and Billy Blunt each knew that they had been very important indeed in helping to give Mr Rudge a really proper Blacksmith's Wedding!

Milly-Molly-Mandy and Guy Fawkes Day

Once upon a time Milly-Molly-Mandy and some of the others were coming home from school one afternoon. It was getting dusk, and fallen leaves were chasing each other along the road.

When they came to Miss Muggins' shop Milly-Molly-Mandy and little-friend-Susan and Billy Blunt stopped a moment to look in Miss Muggins' shop-window. Miss Muggins' shop mostly sold uninteresting things, like stockings and dusters and baby-clothes. But it sold some interesting things too, like sweets and toys and pencil-cases. So it was worth looking in sometimes to see of there was anything worth looking at.

And – do you know! – there *was* something! There was a bright-pink cardboard face with slits for eyes, and a box full of blue and red sticks and curly things of odd sizes.

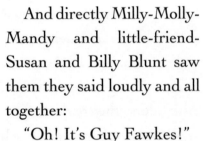

And directly Milly-Molly-Mandy and little-friend-Susan and Billy Blunt saw them they said loudly and all together:

"Oh! It's Guy Fawkes!"

They weren't sure when the Fifth of November was, but of course it must be soon, what with the dark afternoon and the fallen leaves and those things in Miss Muggins' shop window.

"We ought to have a guy with a horrid face on it!" said Milly-Molly-Mandy.

"We ought to have a big bonfire and dance round it!" said little-friend-Susan.

"We ought to buy some fireworks," said Billy Blunt.

"Let's start saving our pocket-money and collecting things for Guy Fawkes day!" said Milly-Molly-Mandy.

So, to begin with, they all went along together to the nice white cottage with the thatched roof (where Milly-Molly-Mandy lived) for Milly-Molly-Mandy to ask if they might start making a bonfire out in the yard for Guy Fawkes night.

Father said: "Go ahead. I'll be sawing some dead branches off the big walnut-tree soon, which you can have for it."

Mother said: "Here's an old hat of Father's which looks about right for a guy!"

Grandpa said: "I've torn my old raincoat on the gate and I'm afraid it's past mending now. You'd better have that too."

Grandma said: "Take it, quick, Milly-Molly-Mandy, before he changes his mind. I'm tired of trying to patch it."

Uncle said: "I suppose you'll be wanting some squibs to make me jump. Here's a shilling for you."

Aunty said: "I'll say this for Guy Fawkes day – it gives you a chance to get rid of the rubbish!" And she handed over a pair of gardening-gloves with the fingers in holes.

Milly-Molly-Mandy and little-friend-Susan and Billy Blunt were very pleased.

They went out into the yard to decide where to have the bonfire, and Billy Blunt carried the old hat and coat and gloves, which were exactly right for a guy. "I'd better take these home and put them in our

There was a bright-pink cardboard face

shed," said Billy Blunt. "They'll be safer there."

Then he and little-friend-Susan had to hurry off to their teas, and Milly-Molly-Mandy went in to hers.

For the next week or so after school they were all very busy collecting firewood. It was quite hard work to find enough for a really big bonfire. They lugged home fallen branches and bundles of twigs and baskets of fir-cones from the woods and hedges. Sometimes they found bits of loose fencing too, but they knew they mustn't take those, so they always tried to fix them back in place (because, of course, you mustn't let cows and sheep get out to wander on the road or lose themselves).

They clubbed together and bought the horridest pink cardboard face in Miss Muggins' shop, and as many squibs as they could get for their money. Billy Blunt had

charge of these (because you could trust
Billy Blunt not to let them off before the
time). He took charge of making the guy
too, as he had its clothes, and he promised
to bring it along on the Fifth, ready for the
burning.

Soon the bonfire had grown to a fine,
great heap, so that only Father or Uncle
could add things to it, because nobody else
could reach high enough.

And then on Guy Fawkes day – would you believe it! – it *rained*.

Going to school, Milly-Molly-Mandy and little-friend-Susan and Billy Blunt did hope it would stop in time for the bonfire that evening. It wasn't far for little-friend-Susan to come from the Moggses' cottage, but it was quite a walk for Billy Blunt, right down in the village.

"We wouldn't want to light the bonfire if you couldn't come, Billy," said Milly-Molly-Mandy.

"We'd have to have it to-morrow instead," said little-friend-Susan.

"Wouldn't be Guy Fawkes day to-morrow," said Billy Blunt. (Which was quite true.)

"You've got our fireworks, don't forget," said Milly-Molly-Mandy.

"And our guy, remember," said little-friend-Susan.

"Don't you worry," said Billy Blunt.

But you never knew – mothers often got fussy over your going out on rainy evenings, getting school clothes wet and that sort of thing.

When Milly-Molly-Mandy got home that afternoon she hoped Mother wouldn't notice her wet coat when she took it off. But Mother did. And she hung it up in the kitchen to dry, and her hat and rubber boots too.

"They're sopping, Milly-Molly-Mandy," said Mother. "We shall only just get them dry enough for you to wear to school tomorrow."

Milly-Molly-Mandy's heart sank.

"But what about going out to the bonfire to-night?" she asked.

"We shall have to think about that," said Mother. "Call the others in to tea now, Milly-Molly-Mandy."

During tea (Milly-Molly-Mandy had a little brown egg with hers) she suddenly wondered out loud: "Why do we have Guy Fawkes day, and burn him?"

Father said: "Don't you know? He was a real live person once."

Mother said: "He tried to blow up Parliament with gunpowder years and years ago."

Grandpa said: "Just when the King and important people were coming to open it."

Grandma said: "But they found out just in time, and he and his bad friends were punished."

Uncle said: "And now you kids want to blow us all up with your squibs and bonfires to celebrate him."

Aunty said: "No, it's because they are so glad Parliament was saved!"

"Well," said Milly-Molly-Mandy, sucking her egg-spoon, "I'm glad Guy Fawkes didn't manage to blow up anything. But I don't think I want our guy to be burnt – *he* hasn't done anything naughty!" And then she asked, "Have you thought about what I can wear when we burn the bonfire to-night?"

So directly tea was over Mother got an old jacket of her own and put it on Milly-Molly-Mandy (she had to tuck the cuffs up a lot). And she wrapped an old shawl round Milly-Molly-Mandy's head and shoulders. And she put her own goloshes over Milly-Molly-Mandy's shoes and tied them on with string.

Milly-Molly-Mandy looked like a proper little guy herself!

Then there came a tapping on the back door. And in shuffled little-friend-Susan, in her father's water-proof cape (which came down below her knees) and her mother's rubber boots (which came nearly up to her knees) and her own pixy hood.

Little-friend-Susan looked a proper little guy too!

Even Toby the dog barked at them. (But he wagged his tail too.)

Then both the little guys shuffled outside to look for Billy Blunt. It was dark and wet, but not actually raining now, and it felt very exciting to be out.

"I do hope his mother lets him come," said Milly-Molly-Mandy.

"So do I," said little-friend-Susan. "He's got all our things."

But they couldn't see him coming along

the road, so they shuffled round to the yard to look at their bonfire.

Father and Uncle were both there with a lantern, and just as they came up Father put a match to a rocket fixed to a fence-post. There was a great *bang!* and a *whoosh!* and showers of beautiful stars lit up everything.

Milly-Molly-Mandy and little-friend-Susan shrieked with excitement, and Milly-Molly-Mandy cried, "Oh, I wish Billy Blunt would come quickly!"

And then, suddenly, they saw the guy!

It was sitting on the bonfire heap – a

splendid guy, with a horrid pink cardboad face, and a dirty old hat and raincoat, and ragged gloves at the end of its stiff, sticking-out arms.

Milly-Molly-Mandy and little-friend-Susan shrieked again with excitement, and they looked about everywhere for Billy Blunt (because, of course, they knew the guy couldn't have got there by itself).

Uncle hung the lantern on the barn door, and they searched in the barn, and round the cowshed. But they couldn't see Billy Blunt.

"Well," said Father;

"we'd better get your bonfire going now, and not wait any longer."

"Oh, don't burn the guy yet!" said Milly-Molly-Mandy. "Let's save it – perhaps Billy Blunt will come."

It looked such a horrid guy, with its pink grinning face. She didn't like to reach up and touch it to push it out of the way. But Uncle said loudly:

"Oh, let's burn it up and get it done with!" And he struck a match.

And then – what DO you think happened?

The guy suddenly threw up its tattered gardening-glove hands, and it jumped down off the bonfire to the ground in a great hurry, all by itself!

You should have heard Milly-Molly-Mandy's and little-friend-Susan's shrieks!

Then the pink cardboard mask fell off and rolled on the ground, and they saw some one else's face grinning at them under the guy's shabby old hat.

"It's Billy Blunt!" shrieked Milly-Molly-Mandy, catching hold of his ragged old coat.

"It's Billy Blunt!" shrieked little-friend-Susan, picking up the cardboard mask and trying it on herself.

"*Boo!*" shouted Billy Blunt, waving his arms. But he couldn't frighten them any more, now that they knew who it was.

So then he told them how his mother hadn't wanted him to come out and get his school clothes wet again, and how he had taken the old hat and coat off the guy he had made and put them on himself instead. So then Mrs Blunt had let him come along and pretend to be the guy.

"Huh! Frightened you girls properly, didn't I?" said Billy Blunt, grinning, as he handed them their share of squibs out of his coat-pockets.

"You were frightened too, properly, when you thought Uncle was going to light the bonfire!" said Milly-Molly-Mandy.

"Serve you right for frightening us so!" said little-friend-Susan.

Then Uncle really put a match to the bonfire, and it began to blaze up. And Father let off some more rockets. And Grandpa and Grandma and Mother and Aunty came out to watch (leaving Toby the dog and Topsy the cat safely shut indoors, lest they should get scared at the noise and run away). And Milly-Molly-Mandy and little-friend-Susan and Billy Blunt lit their squibs, which cracked and banged and made Uncle jump so much that they laughed and laughed!

And what with the roaring of the bonfire and the banging of the fireworks and the shouts of Milly-Molly-Mandy and little-friend-Susan and Billy Blunt, anyone would know they had a splendid Guy Fawkes celebration, even though they didn't burn the guy.

But that, said Father, was because it was really too difficult to choose, with *three* guys jumping round and round the bonfire!

Anyhow, they burnt the guy's dirty old hat and gloves. But his raincoat Mrs Blunt had to put into the dustbin as soon as Billy Blunt got home again that evening after the bonfire was out!

Milly-Molly-Mandy Helps to Thatch a Roof

Once upon a time it was a very blustery night, so very blustery that it woke Milly-Molly-Mandy right up several times.

Milly-Molly-Mandy's little attic bedroom was just under the thatched roof, so she could hear the wind blowing in the thatch, as well as rattling her little low window, and even shaking her door.

Milly-Molly-Mandy had to pull the bedclothes well over her ears to shut out some of the noise before she could go to sleep at all, and so did Father and Mother and Grandpa and Grandma and Uncle and Aunty, in their bedrooms. It was so very blustery.

The next morning, when Milly-Molly-Mandy woke up properly, the wind was still very blustery, though it didn't sound quite so loud as it did in the dark.

Milly-Molly-Mandy sat up in her little bed, thinking, "What a noisy night it was!" And she looked toward her little low window to see if it were raining.

But what do you think she saw? Why, lots of long bits of straw dangling and swaying just outside from the edge of the

thatched roof above. And when she got up
and looked out of her little low window
she saw – why! – lots of long bits of straw
lying all over the grass, and all over the
flower-beds, and all over the hedge!

Milly-Molly-Mandy   stared   round,
thinking, "It's been raining straw in the
night!"

And then she thought some more. And
suddenly she said right out loud, "Ooh!
The wind's blowing our nice thatched roof
off!"

And then Milly-Molly-Mandy didn't
wait to think any longer, but
ran barefooted down into
Father's and Mother's room,
calling out, "Ooh! Father and
Mother! The wind's blowing
our nice thatched roof off, and
it's lying all over the garden!"

Then Father jumped out of

bed, and put his boots on his bare feet, and his big coat over his pyjamas, and ran outside to look. And Mother jumped out of bed, and wrapped the down-quilt round Milly-Molly-Mandy, and went with her to the window to look (but there wasn't anything to see from there).

Then Father came back to say that one corner of the thatched roof was being blown off, and it would have to be seen to immediately before it got any worse. And then everybody began to get dressed.

Milly-Molly-Mandy thought it was kind of funny to have breakfast just the same as usual while the roof was blowing off. She felt very excited about it, and ate her porridge nearly all up before she even remembered beginning it!

"When shall you see to the roof?" asked Milly-Molly-Mandy. "Directly after breakfast?"

And Father said, "Yes, it must be seen to as soon as possible."

"How will you see to it?" asked Milly-Molly-Mandy. "With a long ladder?"

And Father said, "No, it's too big a job for me. We must send for Mr Critch the Thatcher, and he'll bring a long ladder and mend it."

Milly-Molly-Mandy felt sorry that Father couldn't mend it himself, but it would be nice to see Mr Critch the Thatcher mend it.

Directly after breakfast Aunty put on her hat and coat to go down to the village with the message; and Milly-Molly-Mandy put on her hat and coat and went with her, because she wanted to see where Mr Critch the Thatcher lived. And as they went out of the gate the wind got another bit of thatch loose on the roof, and blew it down at them; so they hurried as

fast as they could, along
the white road with the
hedges each side, down
to the village.

But when Aunty
knocked at Mr Critch
the Thatcher's door (he
lived in one of the little
cottages just by the pond

where the ducks were), Mrs Critch, the
Thatcher's wife, opened it (and her apron
blew about like a flag, it was so windy).

And Mrs Critch, the Thatcher's wife,
said she was very sorry, but Mr Critch had
just gone off in a hurry to mend another
roof, and she knew he would not be able
to come to them for a couple of days at the
earliest, because he was so rushed – "what
with this wind and all," said Mrs Critch.

"Dear, dear!" said Aunty. "Whatever
shall we do?"

Mrs Critch was sorry, but she did not know what they could do, except wait until Mr Critch could come.

"Dear, dear!" said Aunty. "And meantime our roof will be getting worse and worse." Then Aunty and Milly-Molly-Mandy said good morning to Mrs Critch, and went out through her little gate into the road again.

"Father will have to mend it now, won't he, Aunty?" said Milly-Molly-Mandy.

"It isn't at all easy to thatch a roof," said Aunty. "You have to know how. I wonder what we can do!"

They set off back home along the white road with the hedges each side, and Aunty said, "Well, there must be a way out, somehow." And Milly-Molly-Mandy said, "I expect Father will know what to do."

So they hurried along, holding their hats on.

As they passed the Moggses' cottage they saw little-friend-Susan trying to hang a towel on the line, with the wind trying all the time to wrap her up in it.

Milly-Molly-Mandy called out, "Hullo, Susan! Our roof's being blown off, and Mr Critch the Thatcher can't come and mend it, so Father will have to. Do you want to come and see?" Little-friend-Susan was very interested, and as soon as she had got the towel up she came along with them.

When Father and Mother and Grandpa and Grandma and Uncle heard their news they all looked as if they were saying, "Dear, dear!" to themselves. But Milly-Molly-Mandy looked quite pleased, and said, "Now you'll have to mend the roof, won't you Father?"

And Father looked at Uncle, and said, "Well, Joe. How about it?" And Uncle said, "Right, John!" in his big voice.

And then Father and Uncle buttoned their jackets (so that the wind shouldn't flap them), and fetched ladders (to reach the roof with), and a rake (to comb the straw tidy with), and wooden pegs (with which to fasten it down). And then they put one ladder so that they could climb up *to* the thatched roof, and another ladder with hooks on the end so that they could climb up *on* the thatched roof; and then Father gathered up a big armful of straw, and he and Uncle set to work busily to mend the hole in the thatch as well as they could, till Mr Critch the Thatcher could come.

Milly-Molly-Mandy and little-friend-Susan, down below, set to work busily to collect the straw from the hedges and the flower-beds and the grass, piling it up in one corner, ready for Father when he came down for another armful. And they helped to hold the ladder steady, and handed up sticks for making the pattern round the edge of the thatch, and fetched things that Father or Uncle called out for, and were very useful indeed.

Soon the roof began to look much better.

Then Father fetched a big pair of shears, and he snip-snip-snipped the straggly ends of the straw all round Milly-Molly-Mandy's little bedroom window up under the roof. (Milly- Molly-Mandy thought it was just like the nice white cottage having its hair cut!) And then Father and Uncle stretched a big piece of wire netting over the mended place, and fastened it down with pegs. (Milly-Molly-Mandy thought it was just like the nice white cottage having a hair-net put on and fastened with hairpins!)

And then the roof was all trim and tidy again, and they wouldn't feel in any sort of a hurry for Mr Critch the Thatcher to

Soon the roof began to look much better

come and thatch it properly.

"Isn't it a lovely roof?" said Milly-Molly-Mandy. "I knew Father could do it!"

"Well, you can generally manage to do a thing when you have to, Milly-Molly-Mandy," said Father, but he looked quite pleased with himself, and so did Uncle.

And when they saw what a nice snug roof they had now, so did Mother and Grandpa and Grandma and Aunty and Milly-Molly-Mandy!

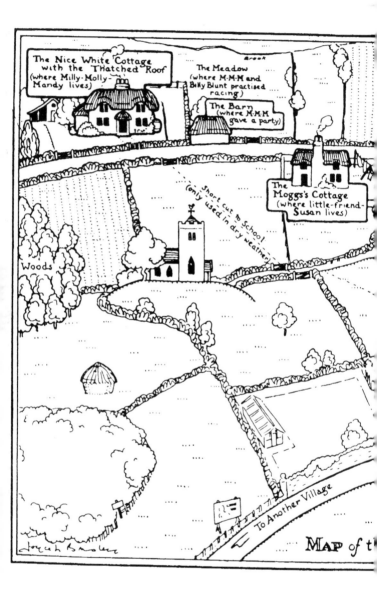